FALLING

INTO

PLACE

A Novella

ELAINE L. ORR

DEDICATION

To all who served, but especially those who were changed by their time in the military.

And their families.

ACKNOWLEDGMENTS

Thanks to the Decatur, Illinois "Write Stuff" Critique Group, whose members are generous with their time and tough with their comments.

My perspective was informed by photos my father, Msgt. Miles D. Orr, took in Africa during World War II – such as this one.

CHAPTER ONE

IF YOU STARED AT THEM
long enough, the red petals blended
into one another. The flower stems
bent slightly in the arid breeze and
the grey stones, pebbles really,
looked almost as thirsty as the small
plant. Though others might find the
picture stark, Everett cherished it.
He could almost feel the calm that

the first view of a poppy field had brought him.

As they got things ready for a rummage sale a couple months earlier, Leslie had suggested selling the painting. She thought it had grown dingy, with dust that had seeped onto the matting because of the loose frame. Before he could protest, Sue Ellen had proclaimed it a special painting, and Myra had volunteered to reframe it for him. Now, dusted and with sparkling glass, it looked as beautiful as it did when Everett had hung it many years before.

The four children were on their own, had been for years. Though Everett missed hearing them play or describe some project, his two daughters and sons Gerard and Stephen were always in his heart.

They kept tabs on Sue Ellen. Stephen stopped by every evening on his way home from work. Leslie in the morning, Myra at lunch. Gerard called. They monitored her more strictly than she had watched over them, which was saying a lot.

They also seemed to need to tell her of their successes in school, at work, or in whichever sport they were playing at the moment. They were as athletic as adults as they had been as children.

Sue Ellen had seen to that. She had been assistant coach of the girls' softball team when Leslie was in fourth grade. She coached the next year. Sue Ellen's role marked the first time a county softball team had a woman coach.

That same year Everett's blue roses had bloomed for the first time. He had checked them every morning when he watered them, and again each afternoon, just before the children's games. He would have looked at them constantly, but Sue Ellen didn't like him to be in the yard all day. She didn't mind that she had to teach school even when the children were young, didn't mind that he simply stopped working. She did mind if the neighbors saw him in the front yard when men were supposed to be at work.

So he stayed inside or in his back garden. He always did the dishes from breakfast and dinner. But he didn't cook. There were too many ingredients to get together at the same time, especially when you were cooking dinner for so many people. He did put out the cereal bowls for breakfast.

SUE ELLEN'S STEP ON THE STAIRS made Everett turn. She was thinner than she had been a year ago, but other than that it was impossible to tell how sick she had been. "Ready?" he asked.

"Oh, yes. Anything to make Dr. Markham happy." She scrunched her face at him, as if she had just taken some ill-tasting medicine.

Everett shook his head. "Just so you don't give him that look. He did save your life, you know."

Sue Ellen laughed in the almost carefree manner she had acquired since her recovery. "I won't. I'm going for this check-up to please you and Dr. Markham, and I plan on being polite to both of you."

As she backed the car out of the driveway, Everett surveyed the largest flowerbed in the front yard. June had brought a riot of color to the bed of annuals. It took the most planning and labor each year. Maybe that's why it was always his favorite bed.

This year, the begonias were the brightest red he could remember, and the geraniums had spread out so much that he realized he would have to trim them to keep them from throwing too much shade on the bright yellow marigolds in front. Who ever heard of trimming back geraniums?

EVERETT HAD BROUGHT his copy of *Gardening Today* to read while he waited for Sue Ellen to get her CAT scan. Myra had given him the subscription every year for Christmas since she first started working. He always read it, though it was written more for someone who wanted to minimize the time they spent to get a lush summer garden.

He closed it as Sue Ellen came back into the waiting room. She stopped to ask the receptionist about her infant daughter. They had struck up a friendship last year. Everett knew that talking to the young woman about the impending birth had been the one source of pleasure in the many visits of a year ago. That was Sue Ellen, at ease with anyone.

"How'd it go?" he asked, as she settled in the chair next to him.

"Piece of cake. All you have to do is keep from sneezing, so they don't have to start over." She pulled a small piece of needlework from her bag.

Everett glanced at it; another Christmas ornament, maybe a Santa. He looked again. It seemed to be Santa's backside. "Is that what I think it is?"

"Everyone does the front. I figured, why not? No pattern though, so I had to design my own." She gave him a sly look, not fully turning her head, to gauge his reaction.

"His boots are backwards."

Sue Ellen gave a startled look at the work in her lap. "Oh, you."

Everett smiled and went back to his magazine. It had taken him years to be able to respond easily to her humor. He liked it, always had, but it was so different from the formality of his own family. Fortunately, all four of the children had inherited her quick wit, though

Leslie had some of his own mother's ability to worry too much.

They sat in easy silence until the nurse called Sue Ellen to talk to the doctor. Everett should have realized when she called to him to come, too, that the news was not going to be good.

Last year, the doctors thought the operation had found all the cancer. This year, they found they were wrong.

EVERETT MOVED HIS CHAIR closer to Sue Ellen's hospital-style bed, now the centerpiece of their dining room. She had wanted it in their bedroom, probably thinking she would be too much the center of attention on the first floor.

Everett's assurance that there would be more room for the children to visit in the dining room had not changed her mind. Myra's point that he would probably fall down the stairs if he went up and down ten times a day had convinced Sue Ellen that the dining room furniture would be easy to store in the garage.

Sue Ellen turned her head, and Everett rose slowly to look at the tube that stretched from the small bag of liquid food into the surgically made hole in her stomach. Sometimes there was an air bubble in the narrow tube. Not that Sue Ellen could tell. He would notice and tap on the line, and she would thank him, as if he had served her pumpkin pie instead of the yellowish liquid that had kept her sated since she'd lost so much of her colon to cancer.

She opened her eye. "Did you check the time?"

"I did. It's set."

She wanted him to learn to cook. He would never learn her recipes, but she insisted on teaching. It was important to her, so he listened carefully, tried to follow her instructions.

"When the bell goes off, you add the mushrooms. Those are the last thing." Her eyes met his as she spoke, and the look was as firm as if she'd been asking him to move his potting soil off the back steps so he wouldn't track dirt into the house.

"The mushrooms. I remember." Her spaghetti sauce had more ingredients than a mixed seed packet had flower varieties.

He patted Sue Ellen's hand and walked the short distance to the kitchen to inspect the timer, one of the old-fashioned wind-up kind. The device on the stove required so many choices. Did you want to start timing now, or later? In the AM, or PM?

The wind-up timer was white, with numbers etched in faded red around the dial. Sue Ellen kept it in the cupboard with the spices. She used it at Thanksgiving and Christmas, when she had lots of things cooking at once. Everett had retrieved it and put it on the stove.

Not near the burners, where it would melt, but on the top of the stove, above the clock.

Two minutes more before he was to add the mushrooms. He opened the refrigerator and took them out. He had already washed them and sliced off the tips. They were so pliable, unlike the celery he had added earlier, which fought every pare of the knife. The twelve capped fungi were large and firm. He still had to slice them lengthwise. If it were up to him, they'd go in whole. Easier to spear with a fork when it came time to eat.

In the foyer, the front door opened. "Mom?"

The timer dinged, and Everett lifted the lid from the simmering pot of sauce.

"Did you hear that?" Sue Ellen asked.

"Hi, Dad," Stephen called to him.

"I'll add the mushrooms." He placed the pot lid upside down, so it rested on its round handle. Flecks of sauce dotted the inside of the lid, and he admired the pattern.

Leslie did the shopping now. They thought he couldn't do it. Perhaps he would surprise her next week. When Stephen came, he would say he was going out for a few minutes. He would walk to the convenience store two blocks away and buy...what? Bread and soup. Sue Ellen liked tomato soup.

What was he thinking? She couldn't eat the soup. And he didn't even like it. Didn't really like the spaghetti sauce all that much, though he had always eaten it. He sliced the last mushroom and carefully placed the knife in the sink.

"Dad." Stephen appeared in the door of the small kitchen. "You need anything?"

"Not a thing. The nurse comes tomorrow."

Stephen merely nodded. Of course, Everett thought, he would know that. Their children were all as good as Sue Ellen was at keeping schedules straight.

Everett was not. However, there was not too much to remember these days. The hospice nurse came on Monday, Wednesday and Friday. The nurse's aide came Monday through Saturday. Apparently, you weren't supposed to be sick on Sunday, because no one came.

"I'll see you tomorrow evening, then. If you think of anything you need me to pick up, you can call me at work you know."

As he stirred the sauce, Everett heard Stephen tell his mother good-bye. But she wanted to know about an inventory system he was designing at work. He described a problem with the computer program, and then the front door opened and shut quickly as Stephen left.

His older son's career choice still surprised Everett. Stephen had liked to be outdoors, always collected things. Rocks, butterflies, even spiders. When Everett had asked if he was sure he wanted to major in business, Stephen had shrugged and said he had to make a living.

Everett turned off the burner. He would let the sauce cool and then place it in plastic storage containers, date them, and put them in the freezer. Someone would eat it. He would eat a little tonight. Sue Ellen would like that.

Her eyes were closed, but she wasn't asleep. Her skin, always smooth and white, had grown even more pale. The visits wore her out, even the short time the children stayed.

If only he could take her out to the garden. They had a chair on wheels, it even reclined. Everett thought the whole point was to move from the bed, enjoy the sunshine. But she was always too tired. The only time she sat in it was when the aide changed the bed sheets. He would ask her again tomorrow.

Everett picked up the gardening catalog and sat in his customary chair, near the head of her bed. September already. If he didn't order bulbs this week, he wouldn't have them in time to plant.

CHAPTER TWO

WHEN THE NURSE'S AIDE CAME, Everett had at first stayed nearby, in case the woman needed any help. Not that he knew anything about bathing a sick adult. But he did know where the spare towels were kept.

After a few days, he began the trek to the garden. Partly, he left so that Sue Ellen could have some privacy. He realized she was being so careful not to cry out when the woman rolled her from one side to another.

The aide wasn't rough. Sue Ellen had gotten so thin. At least that seemed to be why she was so sore. Everett wanted her to be able to moan if she needed to. It was the least he could do.

The morning dew had been heavy. His roses, already drooping from the shorter ration of sunlight, leaned closer to the ground. Gently he shook the petals of his favorite hybrid. *Sue Ellen Blue,* he called it. He had worked for four seasons to get the perfect shade. She had been delighted.

The back door opened and he recognized Leslie's footstep on the stoop. A heavier step now that she was pregnant again.

"Dad? You in your gardens?"

Where else would he be? "Just here." He stood up straight so she could see him. It used to be the entire back yard was visible from the back deck. Now, the fruit trees blocked the view in a few places.

Leslie walked down the few steps to join him. She was six months pregnant. Like her mother, she carried her pre-natal cargo low.

She bent over to smell the blue roses. "Is the aroma stronger in the early fall, or is it just my imagination?"

Everett nodded. "Your nose tells you the truth. Your mother said when fall came she missed the smell of roses, so I tried to breed it so it would have its strongest scent as the others lost theirs."

Leslie stood back up and stared at him. Usually Everett was comfortable with his oldest daughter, but today he sensed her uneasiness and let it migrate to him.

"Something on your mind, Missy?"

She smiled slightly at the name he had called her since the day she was born. "Dad, we've been talking."

We. It always meant the four of them. His children were a strong team. Sue Ellen saw to that.

"About anything in particular?" He tried to smile as he said it, and must have succeeded, because she seemed to loosen up a little.

"Yes." She placed both hands on her hips and arched her back. Leslie said she carried her baby so low its head must rest on the small of her back. She stretched a lot.

"Well, at least Myra and I have been talking." Leslie looked directly at him. "How do you think it will be with Mother gone?"

"Lonely." Everett thought about it often. They didn't talk so much. Even after she retired from teaching Sue Ellen still had her clubs and hobbies. They took her away during the day almost as much as when she worked. But each night they watched the news together and listened to each other's breathing. For thirty-one years.

He realized Leslie was staring at him. How long had he been looking absently at the roses? "But you don't need to worry about me. Your mother's teaching me to cook, you know."

Leslie's face relaxed into a smile. "So I heard. How's it going?"

Everett shrugged. "I know what I need to know to get by. I'll probably never know everything your mother thinks I should."

Her smile faded, and he wondered what he had said to disappoint her. "My tastes are," he paused, searching for a word, "plainer than your mother's. I like chicken noodle soup. With crackers."

Leslie walked back to the stairs and sat on the second one from the bottom. She patted a spot next to her. "Have a seat, Dad."

Everett held onto the handrail as he eased himself onto the step. All the years of stooping and kneeling in his gardens were beginning to take a toll on his knees. "What makes you so serious, Missy?"

She placed a hand over his, which rested on his knee. "How do you feel about being here by yourself after...you know. When Mom's gone."

So that's what she and Myra had been talking about. "I'll miss her, but I'll be all right." Leslie's expression told Everett that didn't seem to be what she needed to hear, so he went on. "I've been washing the loads of towels for years. Now I do all the laundry." He winked at her. "Eventually I catch on, you know."

Leslie stared straight ahead. "There's more to keeping up a house than loads of laundry, Dad."

Everett looked at the apple tree. Several spots needing pruning before winter. "Your mother's been teaching me what she thinks I need to know. I won't do it as well as she does it, but I'll get by."

He could tell what he said seemed to make her more anxious. Why couldn't he seem to ease her worries?

She drew a breath. "What about the new apartments? You know, the ones near the grocery store."

New apartment house? He had ridden to the store with Sue Ellen many times in the past year. She had been determined to teach him to shop. There had been a big construction site near the store. But since Sue Ellen had been in bed most of the time, Leslie bought the groceries. Apparently the construction had turned into apartments.

"Move there? Why would I do that? My garden is here." He stopped for a moment. Leslie and her husband had a small townhouse, and the second baby would join them and little Jessie May in a few months. "Did you and Jimmy want to move in here, Missy?"

"No!" Leslie dropped his hand and put her own on her stomach.

"We're fine where we are. For now, anyway. It's just..."

Her voice trailed off, and Everett studied her profile as Leslie stared at the apple tree. Her pale skin was framed with auburn hair that today she had swept into a loose French twist. He could hear her as a little girl trying to convince Sue Ellen to let her wear her hair long.

"Too much work, young lady," Sue Ellen would say. "I have my hands full as it is."

Leslie would promise to comb every tangle herself, but Sue Ellen stood her ground. She always did.

Everett took the hand that now rested in Leslie's lap. "Missy, I couldn't live in an apartment. What would I do all day?"

Leslie's dark green eyes met his. "You read, Dad. Every night. And you like the old movies."

"I read seed catalogs and books on landscaping more than anything else." He squeezed her hand. "I was thinking of putting a new rose garden on the side yard. It would..." Her expression stopped him.

"But Dad, do you really think you can manage?"

Her question surprised him. He might have expected Myra or Gerard to think he functioned at such a low level that he couldn't get on by himself. But Leslie. She could remember when he worked, couldn't she?

"I need to stay with my gardens, Missy. I'll get by just fine." He stood and nodded toward the apple tree. "It will all work out."

Leslie stared at the tree and said nothing. After a few moments she stood, leaning on the side rail of the steps as she did. "We'll see how it goes, Dad."

AFTER SHE LEFT, Everett walked toward the back of the nearly one-acre garden. When they bought the house, it had been at the edge of town. Not even any sidewalks. Their friends had poked fun at them for buying so far from the grocery store.

Now, every few months someone approached them about subdividing their lot so they could build a house in such a 'close-in' neighborhood. Their friends had long since moved even further away from the center of town, anxious to avoid congestion.

He bent to pull a weed in the middle of the gladiola bed. The tall, late-blooming flowers had been in this spot since the first year they moved in. He had started the first of them in pots on the balcony of their small apartment.

They were married in June 1946, the first spring after the final end of the war, along with half of Burlington, Iowa. The influx of returning GIs and the dozens of marriages had created a housing shortage in the town. He and Sue Ellen had been happy to have their cramped quarters.

The two-room apartment was meant to hold him and Sue Ellen, but baby Leslie had come sooner than they had planned. Her bassinet just fit into the corner of their bedroom. On warm days, when he got home from work, Everett wheeled it onto the balcony. The three of them watched the sun set over the Mississippi River.

After the war, the GI bill paid for him to go through the electrician program. He had thought about taking something in horticulture, but he had to agree with Sue Ellen. What would he do with it? He had some ideas, but mostly they involved building a greenhouse. That cost money.

The electrical work wasn't so bad. He liked wiring the new houses. Every day people would flip a switch and light up their home, all because of his work.

"MR. JENKINS. I'M LEAVING NOW." Everett waved at the health aide, who stood on the back deck, and walked toward the house. Sue Ellen told him she didn't need him with her all the time, but he didn't feel right leaving her alone in the house when he was in the warm fall sunshine.

He pulled the screen door shut behind him, careful not to bang it. The last few days, noises bothered Sue Ellen. They used to sit behind the high school band when Gerard played the trombone at football games. The combination of instruments and excited student cheers were no bother. Today, a slammed kitchen cabinet brought a wince.

He could see the aide waiting for the bus in front of the house. She knew he would come in, so she hadn't waited. Good she didn't. As he glanced out the window, the bus pulled to the curb.

Everett walked into the dining room to check on Sue Ellen. Though her eyes were shut, her face was not at peace. The baths were getting harder for her every day.

"Would you like some of your pain medicine?" he asked.

Her eyes opened and she gave him a half smile. "I thought I'd wait until after Myra left."

Everett shook his head. "I know you want to be able to talk to her, but if you wait too long it'll just be harder for the medicine to work." Everett opened the small cabinet and took out the needle he would use to inject the pain medicine into her IV tubing.

"You're the boss." Her voice was almost a whisper.

The boss. Sue Ellen was the boss. Since he'd been at home, anyway. Before that, he was in charge of his own electrician business.

If it hadn't been for the fall, he might have stayed an electrician. Wiring overhead lights for an upstairs wasn't easy. You had to climb around in the attic on joists, rarely floorboard. He did it, of course. It was like the obstacle course he had to run in basic training, except there you stepped between the wood poles on the ground. In houses under construction you stepped on the wood.

He simply forgot where the hole was. The fall to the floor below seemed to take forever. Like the time his bomber had gone into a tailspin. The right propeller quit on him, the mechanic who was supposed to keep the plane in top shape. For thirty long seconds they had plummeted before he and Benny had managed to right the plane. If they had been over a city, they would have been shot down for sure.

Both times he tumbled out of control. This time he did hit the ground. Hit the subflooring on the second floor of that two-story house and gave himself a huge bump on the head and broke his shoulder. The doctor kept talking about how his shoulder broke his fall, or his head would have been hurt a lot worse than a mild concussion.

All Everett wanted to do was get out of that hospital. Get out and go home and rest. Of course, it wasn't quiet at home anymore, but that was all right with him. Leslie was the prettiest baby God ever made. And she loved her daddy. It was hard to keep her from climbing all over Everett while that shoulder healed.

Then the qualms started. That was Everett's word for them, anyway. First, it was just a fear of falling. He dealt with that by hiring a helper, another vet. The helper, Gabe his name was, climbed in the attics or on any ladder higher than a step stool.

The big problems didn't start until Everett became convinced he would be electrocuted. He tried to talk to Sue Ellen about it. But she had her hands full. Leslie was two, and Stephen was just one. And she was pregnant again. They told themselves this would be the last one. They loved their children with

all their hearts, but three was
enough.

Sue Ellen told him everything
would be fine, he was just having a
nervous spell. Everybody had them.
They went away.

Everett's didn't. He had finally
sold his now faltering electrician
business, glad to get at least some
money for it and be away from the
wires. Sue Ellen was angry, but she
finally told him as long as he liked
what he did, that was good enough
for her. He was the one who had to
go to work while she stayed home
with the babies.

And he had tried. For years. The
closest he'd come to a second career
was his job at the hardware store.
They hired him to manage the

garden section, always busy because of new homes going up.

But eventually they wanted him to work in the store. He couldn't stand on the step ladder to arrange goods on top shelves. And he hadn't wanted to learn to drive the truck used to deliver lumber or large items.

In the end, the manager had said he would lay Everett off, so he could collect unemployment. That money gave Sue Ellen time to find a teaching job.

MYRA'S FOOTSTEPS WERE lighter than Leslie's these days. "Hi, guys."

Sue Ellen's expression relaxed into a smile. Everett was glad he had given her the medicine. Her eyes might not be as alert, but their breezy youngest daughter would not have to see her mother in as much pain.

Myra kissed him on the cheek before she bent over her mother. Her light perfume lingered. What flower did it smell like?

"You look great today, Mom." Myra reached for the comb to gently rearrange Sue Ellen's hair. The aide always put a part in it, on the left side. She had always brushed it straight back.

Sue Ellen studied Myra as she combed. "You have a late lunch hour today?"

Myra usually stopped by just after noon, and it was almost one o'clock.

"I took the afternoon off. Have some stuff I have to do." Myra smiled at both parents as she put down the comb.

Why did he think she was hiding something? Myra was their biggest talker, unable to keep a morsel of her life or her opinions from anyone within thirty feet. It was she who told him the zinnias and marigolds made his mid-summer garden look like that of an amateur. "Keep the roses, dahlias, and daisies Pop, and lose the tacky stuff."

He kept them the next year, but in a separate plot along the fence.

When they had little money, the first years after Sue Ellen went back to teaching school, zinnias and marigolds were the only annuals he could afford. He would always plant them.

Myra was in the kitchen now. Since she came each day on her lunch hour, she always fixed herself something. Everett liked that about her. The others worried about eating in front of Sue Ellen, afraid that the odors of what she could no longer ingest would make her unhappy.

"Mom knows we eat, Gerard. Get a grip."

She had a point.

Myra brought her cup of tomato soup into the dining room and chattered away about a brochure she was designing for a new dry cleaning business. She wanted the owner to put more emphasis on the alterations he and his wife did, because then she could include a drawing of a threaded needle poised above what she called a "really fantastic flowered skirt."

Myra loved to put her own artwork in the commercial designs. Sue Ellen thought she knew the new owner's father. Hadn't he coached in the "A" softball league when she did? He had, Myra told her.

Leave it to Sue Ellen to remember.

They finished talking about the brochure, and Myra stood, empty soup mug in hand. "I'm going to run a couple errands and come back later this afternoon." She turned to Everett. "I can sit with Mom if you have stuff to do in the garden."

"That would be great."

She went in the kitchen to rinse out her mug, and Everett inspected the IV tube for bubbles. The nurse explained to him that if the line had a bubble the machine would beep. He liked to check so the machine stayed quiet.

CHAPTER THREE

EVERETT TUGGED GENTLY at the tomato. The weekend would bring a hard frost. He would have to pick the remaining eight or ten tomatoes and put them in a paper sack in the basement. Or he could fry them, like in the movie Sue Ellen liked so much.

Myra's errands had apparently included a trip to the library, because she came back laden with several books and what looked to be colorful brochures. She was probably showing Sue Ellen some of her planned or finished projects.

Whenever Myra left, Sue Ellen used to proudly display her work to Everett. Not that Myra didn't like to show him. Sometimes she did.

The wire stakes around the tomato had come loose, prodded by the plants themselves, as if they sensed this was their last week to stand proudly in the sun. Everett pushed the sharp points into the ground. He leaned on the stake for a moment to be sure its prongs would stay in place.

Jessie May was even more inquisitive about his garden than Gerard had been. He didn't want his four-year old granddaughter to trip over the stake or, more likely, try to pull it the rest of the way out of the ground.

Everett smiled as he thought of her. He and Sue Ellen had taken Jessie to the Iowa State Fair last summer, just the two of them. Sue Ellen had wanted to ride the carousel with the then three-year-old. Leslie and Jimmy had hovered over him as he fastened their daughter into her car seat. As if he and Sue Ellen had never taken care of a toddler together.

It was a good thing they went last year. This year would not have worked.

The door from the kitchen onto the back porch closed with a slam. He would have to let Myra know to be quieter. She waved at him, her arm high above her head, as if she were seeing him off at the train station. Was it only two summers ago that she had taken him and Sue Ellen to the Amtrak depot, so they could go visit Sue Ellen's sister?

Myra walked down the steps, surveying the flower bed closest to the porch as she did so. "What is that new bush, Dad, the one with the pinkish flowers?"

"It was here last year, just didn't bloom long. This is the first year it's had a full growing season." Everett bent over and pulled two red maple leaves that had strayed into the bush. "It's a dwarf butterfly bush. You know how Jessie May likes to look at butterflies. The fragrance is supposed to attract them."

Myra stooped to smell the sole remaining flowering pink spike. "Likes to try to catch them, you mean."

"Never saw her get one yet. Maybe next year." Everett looked at Myra's closely cropped curls as she studied the garden, making a clean visual sweep from one end to the other. She said she would never let her hair grow long because she didn't want it hanging in her face as she drew. Leslie thought Myra should let it grow long and put it in a French braid.

"Listen, Dad." Myra linked her arm in his and guided him to the porch steps. He felt his right shoulder tighten. Leslie had said she and Myra had talked.

"What's on your mind?" He hoped it was something pleasant. Maybe she wanted to pick a large bouquet of flowers to use as a model for one of her paintings. They had created such arrangements together several times. Myra had to be sure the flowers she picked would be available for bouquets over several weeks. She didn't paint quickly.

"I talked to Leslie, Dad."

So, the same topic. "So did I. But, I guess you know that."

Myra smiled. "Do you think we're ganging up on you?"

Everett thought about that for a moment. "Maybe I should wait until I know what you're going to suggest."

She threw back her head and laughed. That was the difference between his two daughters. Whenever they tried to convince him of something, Leslie's brows would furrow and Myra would laugh. Like the time they had taken him shopping for a suit to wear to Leslie's wedding. He couldn't see spending $300 on something he would wear a few times, at most. Myra had told him he could wear it into the hereafter, but that had only upset Leslie. Their compromise was to spend less.

Myra patted his arm before she withdrew hers. "We aren't trying to dictate where you live, Dad. We just worry about you being here by yourself."

Everett looked out over the garden. For the first time, he had planted all pink begonias as border plants. The soft pink color dotted throughout the gardens. Next year he might try something bolder. All red ones, perhaps.

"I've been here since 1949, sweetie. I don't plan to go anywhere else, not as long as I can get up and down these steps by myself." He turned to face her. "I think I'd be a lot more trouble for you if I didn't have my gardens."

He had said the wrong thing. Myra flushed and looked away. "You're no trouble, Dad."

"Not trouble like an ornery child, but I know you wonder how I'll get on after your mother dies." It was the first time he had said that out loud to one of the children.

Sue Ellen insisted that they should avoid the topic, so as not to worry them. As if they didn't know. "The bus stops at the door, you know. I can get where I need to go and buy what I need to use. It even goes within a few blocks of the greenhouse."

Myra smiled. "I can see you trying to load a flat of begonias and a bag of fertilizer onto a city bus."

"Gerard will help me in the spring. He always does."

Myra's expression was hard to read. He didn't like to worry them, but he would never move.

Sue Ellen wouldn't want him to either. Perhaps she could talk to

Leslie and Myra. No, that wasn't fair. Sue Ellen had more than her share to worry about now. But she would want him to stay. Why else would she be teaching him to cook, having him make lists of where all the things were in the kitchen?

"OK, Dad. You've convinced me for now. I can't say Leslie will give up on the idea."

Everett shrugged. "Leslie can talk to me anytime she wants to. She knows that."

Myra kissed his cheek. "And she will."

Everett looked at the dwarf butterfly bush. Leslie's little Jessie May was much more happy-go-lucky than her mother. Leslie and Jimmy were the ones who helped her be that way. If Leslie could just worry less herself.

WHEN MYRA LEFT, Everett took his place near the head of Sue Ellen's bed. She slept peacefully, the pain medicine still doing its work.

Myra had been careful not to close the door hard as she left. She hadn't minded his advice. She never did.

Did he imagine it, or was Sue Ellen's breathing more shallow than it had been? He stood and bent over to study her more closely. The hospice nurse had said her breathing would grow more shallow as 'her time' grew closer. Everett thought that was a ridiculous way to put it. But, he didn't have to talk to people about dying every day.

Though he knew a lot about death.

He decided she was breathing normally. He remembered that when he gave her the pain medicine she sometimes fell into a deep sleep and breathed more softly.

Benny had breathed softly like that, at the end. At first Everett hadn't realized he was hit. They'd been in the foxhole, same as most nights they weren't up in the air. Everett tried to rationalize. If they bombed the Germans, then it made sense that the *Luftwaffe* would try to keep the Americans on the ground.

He and Benny huddled together, the way Everett had seen his sisters with their girlfriends when they had a slumber party. But he and Benny weren't giggling over a secret. They hung onto each other as if the world would end if they let go. Sometimes they'd get worn out from clinging to each other, and they would just lie still.

Wasn't even a bullet that got him. The Germans had come earlier than usual, and the men didn't have everything put away. Later on, they figured a bomb hit directly on the pile of pots and pans the cook had sitting on a table outside the mess tent. A shard of metal tore through Benny's skull. Real quiet like. Everett didn't even know it until he was almost dead.

It was like Benny not to bother anyone when he was dying. Just like Sue Ellen.

CHAPTER FOUR

GERARD CAME SATURDAY MORNING before his softball game. As always, Everett though his son's slight frame gave opponents no clue of how hard he slugged the ball.

Gerard returned late in the afternoon to tell Sue Ellen who had scraped their leg sliding into second base and which of his friends sent best wishes to her.

"So Boomer, he figures he's sure to make it, and he keeps dancing out a few feet from first." Gerard leaned forward, one leg in front of the other and bounced from the ball of one foot to the other.

"But he doesn't know that Martin--he's that guy from the north side who could've had the softball scholarship but wanted to work the farm right away--just got contacts. I mean, none of us knew. Anyway, old Martin fires that ball right to the first baseman, and they box old Boomer in good. Made him mad as a hornet."

Sue Ellen shook her head slightly. "Nicholas always looks for a shortcut."

"Boomer," Gerard stressed his friend's nickname, "plays shortstop mother. There's no such position as shortcut."

"Very funny, young man." Sue Ellen looked to Everett. "When did he get this way?"

"I'm not sure I remember him any other way." Everett looked at his son, who was obviously pleased that he had gotten a light-hearted reaction from his mother.

The footsteps on the front steps sounded like Stephen's. Gerard opened the door before his brother had a chance to. "Stephen. Come on in and hear who else I saw at the games."

"Maybe in a few, Gerard." Stephen crossed the room and leaned over to kiss Sue Ellen gently on the cheek. "Hey mom. You're not believing all of his stories, are you?"

"You're just jealous because that desk job of yours is slowing you down." Gerard made a half-bow. "While I, on the other hand, continue to maintain my fine physique."

"Wait 'til you're thirty, Mr. Potato Head."

Everett had no idea what Gerard had done to earn the title, but he had had it for years and had never liked it.

"Truce. Hey, Pop." Gerard jiggled the keys in the pocket of his jeans. "If Stephen's here for a few, you want me to run you down to the greenhouse for anything?"

Gerard was their most willing errand-runner, and the only one of his children who had the patience to wait while Everett searched the flats of plants for just the right shade of dahlia bulb or the healthiest looking bedding plants.

"When's the last time Dad said no to that?" Stephen asked. "But didn't you just get here?"

"I was here already today, right Pop?" Gerard stood at the foot of Sue Ellen's bed. "You don't mind, do you Mom?"

"Of course not. I'll just rest up for your next story." Sue Ellen's eyes were closed now, but her words were firm.

"Do your thing," Stephen said.

As he went to the kitchen to be sure all the burners were off on the stove, Everett wondered if Gerard had planned to stay only a few minutes. He never seemed to want to sit and talk.

WHEN EVERETT AND GERARD GOT BACK, Jessie May was lying on the front porch, leaning over the edge. She didn't raise her head when she said, "Grandpa, this one's bigger than any of the others."

Everett followed her gaze until he could finally make out the garter snake that was lying on the warm dirt, sunning itself. "I do believe it is."

Jessie twirled a curl, not looking up. "I still don't understand why they don't make good pets."

Gerard sat beside her. "I think it has something to do with pregnant mommies."

As usual, her young uncle could capture her attention even more than a snake. "I don't think the other kinds of mommies like them either."

Gerard tugged on her curl and she swatted at his hand, missing.

He grinned. "Ask Aunt Myra if you can leave it at her house."

Jessie looked at Everett. "Would she let me, really, Grandpa?"

"You better ask her before you try to catch it." Everett put his hand on the door knob. "Have you seen Grandma yet?"

Jessie's eyes went back to the snake. "For a little bit."

"Jessie wants to go to the playground, don't you?" Gerard scooped her up and she squealed in delight.

"I'll tell your mother where you're going -- both mothers. Walk back on the main road, in case Leslie wants to find you."

THE MOOD IN THE DINING ROOM was somber. Stephen sat in a chair on one side of Sue Ellen's bed and Leslie on the other. Everett could tell Leslie had been crying. "Hi, Missy."

She blew her nose. "Hi Dad."

"Gerard and Jessie headed for the playground. Doubt they'll be long." Everett glanced at Stephen who did an almost imperceptible shrug.

Leslie tossed her tissue into a trash can near the head of Sue Ellen's bed. "I wanted Jessie to spend more time with Mom."

Sue Ellen tapped a finger on the bed rail. "You can't force her, sweetie. She'll resent coming over. Resent me."

"How about a coloring book?" Everett asked.

Leslie flushed. "She has several at home."

"I meant put one on the bottom of the bed. She can color while you talk to your mom."

Stephen stood. "Good idea. I'll get one from that play box in the living room."

Sue Ellen turned her head toward Everett. "Crayons are in that bottom drawer in the kitchen."

"Right where you left them," he said.

CHAPTER FIVE

THE RAKE SCRAPED ON the bricks as Everett tried to get the last of the leaves into a pile big enough to scoop into the paper bag. Fall was bestowing them with its presence longer than usual, and Everett considered it a special gift. He didn't mind sitting with Sue Ellen for any time that she was awake, but it was hard to be inside when she slept. And she slept so much more now.

He bent over to grab a small pile of leaves and dusted his hands as he dropped them into the tall recycling bag. A couple more handsful and he would be done. Then he would take the wide push-broom and sweep the brick walkways that wove among the many plant beds that meandered together as his garden.

Sue Ellen used to come outside as he did this. She said it reminded her of how they used to go through the house and tidy up each night after they put the kids to bed. Everett now thought of late October or early November as the time he put his garden to bed for the winter.

He turned to look at the house, expecting to see her on the top deck. How silly. She was there, in a way. He smiled at the thought. Gerard had bought a set of intercoms that you plugged into the wall. One by Sue Ellen's bed, another on the deck.

The outdoor one was set so Everett could listen to her room all the time. Not that he could hear her speak if he was this far away. But he could hear the little bell that Gerard had tied to the railings of the hospital bed. All Sue Ellen had to do was ring it and he would go inside.

He lifted the bag onto the wheelbarrow and placed his rake on top of it. He'd been outside in the beautiful sunlight for almost half an hour. It was time to check on Sue Ellen.

Gerard planned to come by after work today instead of Stephen. Everett wanted to hear about Gerard's meeting with the Zoning Board. He hoped to receive a permit to open a small restaurant on the edge of the old downtown. He believed that if there were a place to eat in that area it would breathe life into the slowly withering neighborhood of brick row houses and small apartment buildings.

The crunch of gravel told him Gerard had pulled into the driveway. Everett parked the wheelbarrow at the bottom of the steps and climbed toward the back door. He had meant to be inside to check on Sue Ellen before Gerard got there. He didn't want one of the kids to find she had died in her sleep.

He walked into the dining room as Gerard came in the front door. They nodded to each other and both looked toward Sue Ellen. She used to wake up when anyone came in the front door, but not now. Not unless it was almost time for the pain medicine to wear off.

"Hi, Pop." Gerard looked at Sue Ellen.

Everett was glad his son had finally gotten better able to deal with his mother's illness. It wasn't easy for any of them, but it was hardest on their youngest son. Sue Ellen said it was because they'd coddled him too much. Maybe.

Everett thought Gerard tuned into others' feelings more than most people. If coddling had created that empathy, that was all right with Everett.

Gerard's forehead wrinkled in a frown. Everett wished he could take away the worry of his children every bit as much as he wished he could take away Sue Ellen's pain. "Sit down, son. Tell us about your zoning meeting."

"Won't we bother Mom?"

"No." Sue Ellen's whisper had a rasp in it Everett hadn't noticed earlier.

He reached over and stroked her hand. "I'm sure she'd like to listen."

Sue Ellen's mouth curved up slightly. Encouraged, Gerard pulled one of the two visitors' chairs closer to the head of Sue Ellen's bed and angled his long body into it. "It went even better than I thought, Mom. They asked lots of questions."

As he talked, Everett checked the tubing that flowed into Sue Ellen's arm. When Gerard left, he would check the stomach tube.

The nurse from the hospice had talked to him and Sue Ellen last week about when to remove it. Things would 'go faster' if they took it out. When she was done explaining what they could expect -- "about four days after the last nourishment and water" -- Everett was glad that Sue Ellen had said she wanted to "wait and see."

He believed the nurse when she said Sue Ellen would be past noticing much at that point, but he could not bear the thought of starving his wife.

The only time he'd been parched and hungry was when Benny forgot to put the water and chocolate bars in the plane. They were returning to the squadron after a bombing raid, heading toward far western Algeria, when they realized they must have been hit in the fuel tank. It couldn't have been a large hole, or they wouldn't have made it as far as they had. They could probably avoid Rommel's troops, but didn't have enough fuel to get back to their desert air base.

Everett could still hear the engines sputter as fuel deserted them. They rolled from side to side, but stayed upright.

Benny did a damn good job landing the plane. The navigator rammed his head against the back of the pilot's seat and was out for about ten minutes, but that was the only injury. The poppy field was a lot softer than crashing on a landing strip, but it wasn't hospitable to airplane tires.

They debated whether to stay with the plane. It would get hot as all get out when the sun came up. But how far would they get walking? Benny had his deck of cards, so worn from all the games of gin and poker that you could almost see through to the numbers. They bet each other the next week's rations of water, chocolate, and, finally, powdered eggs. Everett ended up with all the water, for all the good it did him.

After almost twelve hours, Everett hadn't expected to be rescued. He had decided the high desert was as good as any place to die. Better than in the rubble of the buildings they bombed.

Another plane's navigator had been certain that Everett and Benny's plane had been with the squadron when they turned back toward the air strip. Thanks to his insistence, the Army Air Corps had looked. They were damn lucky.

Luckier than Sue Ellen.

CHAPTER SIX

SUE ELLEN HAD FALLEN asleep by the time Gerard left. Everett studied her cheeks, more sunken and waxy by the day, and decided that it was time for him to start sleeping in the dining room with her. Until now, he had left the portable intercom in the 'on' position in the living room and in their upstairs bedroom; he could hear if she called.

Something told him tonight would be different.

Last week, he had asked Gerard to carry a chaise lounge lawn chair up from the basement, telling him it was in case his knee was stiff. If Leslie and Myra knew Everett thought Sue Ellen was doing so poorly that he planned to sleep downstairs, they would want to be there, too. If he could be certain Sue Ellen would die in the next day or two, he would tell all the children. But, it was only a hunch.

Walking slowly on the steps, he carried two pillows and a blanket downstairs. Next, he retrieved the old sleeping bag from the closet in Stephen and Gerard's bedroom. It would make the lawn chair more comfortable.

As he dropped the pillows on the chair, Sue Ellen opened her eyes. She took in what he was doing, and looked directly at him. "Sleeping with me again, are you?"

He leaned over the bed rail and brushed her hair back. "I thought I might."

"Everett." She closed her eyes, and he waited. "I think it's time to take all the tubes out."

"You sure you're ready for that?"

Her eyes went to the lawn chair again. "I know you're thinking the same thing."

He continued to stroke her hair. "I'll miss you, you know. Who else is going to want to listen to all my ideas for the garden?" He would miss everything about her, but knew that question would please her.

"Try Myra." She met his eyes, and her lips curved slightly.

"She loves the colors, that's for sure." His eyes traveled to the IV tubing. "There's really only this to take out. The feeding tube is empty unless we put something in it."

"Of course." She studied his face intently. "I think you can pull out that needle. You've seen the nurses maneuver them in and out often enough."

"I can, only…the doctor said they would use the IV for strong medicine if you needed it."

"I don't think…I won't need it. The drops under my tongue work fine."

"All right, then." Everett was surprised how calm he felt. Was it always this way when someone died at home instead of in battle?

He studied the IV tube again. "We may not have to take the needle out. I think all I need to do is flip this little plastic switch and it'll stop flowing. Then I can set the bag in your lap."

"You're sure?"

He could tell by her expression that she had made up her mind. "Let's try it. If it's still putting water into you in half an hour, I'll pull the needle." He reached up and turned the tiny plastic knob near the bag of fluid. Sue Ellen's eyes were shut again, so he concentrated on the tube. Sure enough, the dripping stopped within a minute.

He didn't want to make her talk if she needed to rest, so he busied himself with unrolling the sleeping bag and placing it onto the lawn chair. Then he turned on the hallway wall switch to provide light in the dining room, but not too much. Sue Ellen would rest better that way. He wished he had put the lawn chair closer to the bed, but he could do that next time she opened her eyes.

"Everett."

Her voice, stronger than it had been for days, startled him.

"I'm right here."

Her eyes fixed on him intently. "Do we still have that chair on wheels?"

He sensed she was very

determined about something. "Sure do. It's in the living room. Did you want me to sleep in that?" He would do whatever made her happy, of course.

She actually smiled. She was up to something. "I want you to wheel me onto the back porch, so we can look at the garden."

It couldn't be good for her to be outside at dusk at this time of year. With almost a physical jolt, Everett realized that could hardly matter. "I can call Gerard…"

"No, just us." Her eyes were bright. "If you pushed it near the bed, you could help me sit up and kind of slide me into it. We'll put the IV bag on my lap. Like the aide used to do."

Everett looked at her, uncertain what to say.

"Of course," she continued, "you'd have to remember to lock the wheels, or you'll be picking me up off the floor."

"You might be down there a while." He smiled at her, then grew somber again. "Are you sure we can do this?"

"Just lower the bed; I'll be almost even with the chair."

"You must have been thinking about this for a while."

She nodded slightly. "I was just waiting to feel strong enough. I knew I would, one more time."

It took them ten minutes to figure how to actually get Sue Ellen into the chair. Everett wasn't sure which one of them was shaking more. "I'll get you a blanket."

"Bring the medicine, too, okay?" Her voice had lost its earlier strength.

Everett placed a sheet and blanket over her, and put a pillow near each of her hips. She was so thin, he didn't want her to slide too much in the chair.

Slowly he pushed the reclining chair to the back door. She only winced when he tried to ease the chair through the door jamb and brushed against it.

The temperature was still in the mid-50s, so Everett didn't think it would be too cold for her. A light breeze blew the small wind chimes. He rolled the chair closer to the edge of the small deck, and bent over to lock the wheels in place.

"No skydiving tonight?" Her voice had regained some of its strength.

Everett had known the fresh air would be good for her. "Forgot the parachute." He tucked the blanket closer around her.

"Turn on the ground lights, would you? I want to see the mums."

Everett reached just inside the door and flicked the switch. Brilliant hues of yellow, burgundy, and orange seemed to sparkle. He was glad the mums closest to the house were among the most hardy this year.

"Come sit by me."

"Yes, your majesty." Everett slid the canvas deck chair close to her, and saw her lips turn up in a small smile.

"Ok, you can hold my hand, too."

He reached over and took her now angular hand, careful not to grasp it tightly. "Can you see much?"

"I see the beautiful colors. And it smells so wonderful." She turned her head slightly. "Thank you."

"I've wanted to do this for weeks. It's just the kids…"

"They were only trying to help." Her eyes returned to the mums, then scanned the sky. "I was hoping for the moon."

"Maybe later." He stroked the

back of her hand with his thumb. "Do you want some medicine?"

"Very much. I guess the excitement's wearing off."

Everett pulled the small bottle from the pocket of his pants and removed the medicine dropper. "Pretend you're a bird," he said, employing a phrase she had often used with the children when they were still in the high chair.

"Maybe give me just a bit more than usual."

Everett hesitated. He had no idea if the narcotic would hurt her. Realizing the absurdness of his thought, he squeezed more into the dropper. "Okay, just a little more. Don't want an addict on my hands."

"What I really want is a glass of wine, but I don't have anywhere to put it." She opened her mouth and lifted her tongue for the medicine, a twinkle in her eyes.

Everett could tell she was quite pleased with herself. "No seconds." He was finding it hard to continue the lighthearted banter.

She nodded lightly and he sat down and took her hand. His gaze traveled to the edge of the garden. Only a week ago he had seen two deer staring back at him, seemingly trying to discern how to get over the low garden wall. He would never permit them to eat his garden, but he hated the thought of asking the animal warden to remove them. Someone would shoot them if they were taken too far out of town.

He shivered. He had been so concerned about keeping Sue Ellen warm that he had come out in his shirt sleeves. Sue Ellen was asleep now, breathing very shallowly. He decided to go inside to grab a jacket, and call Gerard. There was no way he'd be able to lift Sue Ellen back into bed.

Gerard seemed to think Everett was the one on morphine. Everett had to repeat his request, and assure his son twice that Sue Ellen had wanted to be outside. He did manage to get Gerard to promise not to call Leslie. This was one of those events that would be better for Leslie to hear the day after it happened.

As he walked onto the back deck, Everett said, "Gerard will be..." He stared at Sue Ellen's white face. He had never imagined it would happen so quickly.

CHAPTER SEVEN

IT HAD BEEN EVEN harder than when Benny died. Everett had known it would be, of course. The difference now was that he had his children and Jessie May to think of, and that kept him busy.

Back then, the bombs had nearly destroyed their grouping of tents and dusty runways. Everett had been assigned what the sergeant called scavenger duty. Find anything usable and load it onto one of the six planes they could still fly. He thought of it as salvage duty. Salvage rations, salvage medical supplies, salvage limbs. The sergeant had seemed anxious to keep Everett busy.

Why Sue Ellen and not him? She and Benny were the kind of people who should have lived long lives. Always doing things for others. Well, Everett had too, for many years. Not so much after the qualms started.

"Dad?" Stephen was at his side. "Would you like to come out to talk to people?"

Everett glanced toward the funeral home's view room. "Of course."

Stephen extended his arm, as Everett had often held his out to Sue Ellen.

"Your mother had lots of friends." He stood with his hand on Stephen's arm, but did not link arms with his son. Instead he patted Stephen. "Go visit with your friends. I'm just fine."

As he walked the short distance from the family waiting room to the large funeral home parlor, Everett began to go over the names. Helen Marsh was Sue Ellen's favorite teacher friend, Margaret Simon had been the assistant coach the year the girls' softball team won the county championship. Although he would never remember all of them, he wanted to remember the ones who were most important to Sue Ellen.

He smiled at Myra as he entered

the parlor. She looked calm, the only one of the children who seemed at peace with her mother's death. Myra had sat with her arms around Leslie that first night. Nothing Everett had said comforted his eldest daughter. Thank goodness she had not brought Jessie May to the house.

His granddaughter was here tonight, looking very grown up in a black velvet dress with a white collar and cuffs. Gerard held her as she very seriously explained something to him. "It's not cold when they're down there in the box. It's like it has its own heater."

Gerard's expression was unreadable.

Everett held out his arms as he

walked up, and Jessie swung to him. He winked at her. "That's right. No one is cold after they die."

Jessie nodded. "I don't think Uncle Gerard understands. He was crying."

"Sure he was. I cried some, too, you know." Everett watched her eyes widen. "We'll all miss your Grandma. We know she feels better in heaven, but we still miss her here."

Jessie's stare was impervious. "How can she be in heaven if she's in that box?"

Everett wished the children had gone along with his and Sue Ellen's wish that she, and later he, be cremated. Myra and Stephen and

Gerard had been uncomfortable with it when Sue Ellen talked to them about cremation a few months ago, but had said that they respected Sue Ellen's decision.

Everett should have known that Leslie's silence that night meant that she simply couldn't deal with it. Everett had finally told her that funerals were for the living, and if Leslie did not want her mother cremated, then she would not be. Life insurance would pay for a "real funeral," as Leslie had called it.

"Only her body is in the box. Her heart and soul are in heaven with God." Everett heard the inadequacy of his words. One of the reasons they had wanted cremation was so that Jessie May could be told the Bible quote about people returning to dust.

"How did her heart get out?"

Everett was aware that the soft conversations around him had stopped. "God has very special ways of doing things after people die. We don't understand all of them, but we can always trust Him to do it right."

"Okay," she said.

Everett realized Jimmy was standing next to them.

"Hi Daddy." Jessie pitched herself toward him.

"Whoa, Jess," his son-in-law said. "You have to give Grandpa more warning when you're changing people."

"He's okay with it."

Everett's eyes met Jimmy's and he saw the broad grin there. "Grandpa's okay with whatever you do, Jess. I don't want him to topple over."

"What's topple?" she asked, as Jimmy turned to carry her to where his parents stood.

"That was perfect, Dad." Leslie's red-rimmed eyes were brimming again. "She's been asking me all these questions, and I just didn't know what to say. I don't know what I would do if it weren't for Jimmy."

Everett put his hand on his daughter's shoulder. "You see, Missy, you're the only one who's worried about giving her the wrong answer. As far as Jessie's concerned, any answer you give her is the right one."

He could see Leslie's college roommate walking toward them. "Ask Kathy. She'll tell you a mom's always right."

"That's right, Mr. J." As Leslie almost fell into her good friend's arms, Kathy mouthed a kiss toward Everett.

He winked at her, and made his way to Myra. He and she were to start the guest line. Myra refused to call it a receiving line.

"If we call it that," she had said, "then when I get married someday we'd have to think up a new name for that line." She had made Stephen laugh. That was something.

"Hi, Sweetie." He squeezed her hand. "I'm so glad you wore that purple dress. It was your mom's favorite, you know."

She nodded. "She asked me to wear it. Isn't that wild?"

Her words caught Everett off guard for a moment. He and Sue Ellen had talked about what he would wear (the suit he had worn to Leslie's wedding), but he didn't realize she had talked to the children about this. "That's…good."

After that, it was so busy he had little time to think about anything. Myra, of course, knew everyone's names. He need not have practiced. Though the children were going to take turns standing with him, it was Myra who remained in the guest line most of the night. She seemed to enjoy it.

Sue Ellen always said that Myra was able to 'compartmentalize' the best of all their children. It was an odd expression, but Everett understood what she meant. Myra was no less sad about Sue Ellen's death, but she was able to step away from her grief to greet the dozens upon dozens of people who had come to the funeral home.

Even Gabe, whom Everett had hired to help in his failing electrician business, came. He had aged, but who hadn't?

At some point, a funeral home employee brought Everett a bar stool, a great relief. He could sit but still look people in the eyes. The funeral home staff probably didn't call it a bar stool.

The two hours passed quickly. As it grew closer to nine o'clock, Everett became aware of two men talking to Gerard, and later Gerard and Stephen. One used a cane, but stood ramrod straight. The other was slightly stooped, with hair as white as Sue Ellen's whipped frosting.

He lost sight of them as the choir master from church stood in front of him. Yes, Everett agreed, Sue Ellen had had a beautiful voice.

A few minutes later, the room nearly empty of guests, Gerard and the two men began to walk toward him. Everett gripped his stool. It couldn't be. He didn't want them here.

"Dad," Gerard sounded tentative. Everett seemed to be hearing him through a poor telephone connection. "Dad, these men said they knew you in the war."

Everett stood and, without thinking, saluted Lieutenant Brimmer. What was he doing? He almost had to use his left hand to pull his right hand away from his forehead.

Lieutenant Brimmer looked surprised, then returned the salute. "At ease, corporal."

The other face was grinning at

him. "You old goat. You hated to salute."

Could that white-haired man be Sergeant Melrose? It seemed so.

"I can't believe...What are you...How did you know?" All his questions seemed to run together. Still, they were more orderly than his thoughts.

They had made it home on their own, not in a casket. He had always known that. In fact, Sue Ellen and the lieutenant's wife regularly exchanged Christmas cards. Everett never read them. Sue Ellen understood.

The sergeant's face was serious. "Sue Ellen called us a few months ago. Told us to watch the *Des Moines Register*."

That was why her instructions had included placing a death notice in the Des Moines paper. Everett had assumed it was because her softball team had played all over Iowa. Sue Ellen had hated to hear of someone's death long after it happened. Too late to send a card without opening wounds, she always said.

"I...see. Well, you're here."

Myra took over. "Did you have to drive far?"

Everett did not hear their answer, but was aware that she guided him, the lieutenant, and sergeant to the small grouping of chairs on the far side of the room. He tried to pay attention. They had come a long way. A long way.

The bombing seemed to go on all night. Maybe it did. He lost track of time. They hadn't expected it. Two men were at each anti-aircraft gun, but the Nazis went for them first. No one replaced them.

As he sat clutching Benny, Benny's body, Everett felt himself get hot. He couldn't explain it. The few times he tried to remember what happened next, he wasn't sure what made him crawl out of the foxhole.

The guns were at least forty yards from him. He hadn't really thought about distance, only about getting to the guns to make the bombing stop.

The Army Air Corps gave him a medal, but he'd thrown it away.

That had upset Sue Ellen, and he was really sorry about that. He hadn't meant to distress her. He simply didn't want it in that top drawer, didn't want to be reminded on even those rare occasions when he opened the drawer to get a tie clip.

"Dad?" Myra's voice sounded concerned.

"I'm sorry, sweetheart. I guess I'm tired."

"We should go," Lieutenant Brimmer said.

"Please." Everett finally realized he was supposed to treat them as guests, even if their presence brought back horrible memories. "You must have had a long ride. Would you like to come to the house for coffee?"

Myra beamed at him. Across the room, he could see Leslie and Stephen talking quietly to Gerard. Jimmy was struggling to put a light coat on the nearly asleep Jessie May.

"I'm kinda tired," Sergeant Melrose said. "Hate to admit it, but you gents know I've got a few years on you."

This made Everett smile. The sergeant was in his early thirties back then. The rest of them were at least ten years younger. He had forgotten how they razzed him about that.

"We're staying at the hotel down by the civic center," Brimmer continued. "We should really get some sleep. Early to bed and all that, you know."

Everett stood. "It's really good that you came. Leave it to Sue Ellen."

Sergeant Melrose nodded. "You had a really special one, there, Ev."

It took an interminable amount of time to say goodbye to them. Or so it seemed. Probably less than a minute.

He sensed Gerard at his shoulder and looked up at his suddenly serious son.

"I'm going to drive you home, Dad."

"I thought Myra..."

"Her friend Jeanie drove down from Sioux City, and she has to leave right after the funeral tomorrow. This is the only time they'll get to talk."

"Of course." Everett was glad for any diversions his children could have over the next few days. He wished Leslie would let herself relax with a friend. But that wasn't her way.

As they walked to the door, Everett's eyes strayed to the flowers and he stopped. Red poppies. Who had sent them? He asked Gerard.

"So, they're poppies. It's a pretty flower." Gerard walked to the small plant and looked for the card. "I don't see one. That's funny."

He started to look more, but Everett said it didn't matter. Sue

Ellen had asked someone to send them, he was sure of it.

"YOU WANT TO KNOW WHY I don't talk about it." Everett knew that was the reason Gerard was quiet as he drove.

"I won't ask you, Dad."

"That's good. I'm sorry, Son, but I just can't."

"It really is OK, Dad. Those men..." He stopped. "They said you saved a lot of lives."

"It's what we all did. It's just that..." He stopped. Just what? Just that he couldn't save Benny? That was too simple an answer to why he couldn't talk about it. If that was all it was, it seemed he would have eventually been able to accept it. "I just can't."

"I meant it when I said it was OK. Mom knew. That was enough."

Yes, Everett thought. It was enough.

CHAPTER EIGHT

SUE ELLEN'S IMPECCABLE TIMING failed her in death. It would have been better for Leslie if Sue Ellen hadn't died when Leslie was so pregnant. Sue Ellen didn't plan it that way, and Leslie would have taken her mother's death harder than the other three, no matter when it happened. Or showed it more, anyway.

The weather was warm for mid-December, almost like spring. Everett patted the mulch more firmly around the *Sue Ellen Blue* roses. He was convinced extra mulch let them survive Iowa's cold winters.

If only his oldest daughter could find peace in her mother's quiet death. So many went so violently, before their time.

The ringing of the portable phone startled Everett. He rose from his kneeling position, stumbling slightly on the uneven bricks as his stiff legs were forced into motion faster than he usually permitted.

Gerard had the idea for the phone. Now that Everett was alone in the large house, Gerard wanted him to have a phone within reach all the time. Though he occasionally forgot where he placed the receiver, Everett didn't mind carrying it to the garden. And Gerard called every day.

This time it was Leslie's voice. "Dad, where's Myra?"

Everett had to think for a minute. "In Des Moines. She's presenting..."

"Damn."

"What is it, Missy? Are you all right?"

"I am, dad, but Jessie's not."

Everett fought down the panic. A parent was supposed to stay calm. "What's wrong with her?"

"She's breaking out. The day care center said she has to be picked up. But I can't, of course. And Jimmy had to go to Iowa

City."

She was talking so fast that Everett could barely understand her. She had her car. Or maybe it was in the shop. "Do you need to use Mother's car?"

"I'd catch chicken pox in it as soon as in mine."

Of course, Leslie was the only one who hadn't had chicken pox. Leslie had been exposed as much as the others. Sue Ellen thought she must have been immune. But her upcoming baby didn't need that complication.

"I could take the bus to Jessie's day care and get her." As he said it, Everett wondered how a sick Jessie May would respond to him when she probably wanted her mommy.

Leslie said nothing. He thought she had hung up, and was about to push the off button on his phone when she asked, "Do you have exact change for the bus?"

"I have my senior pass. And I'm sure I'll have change for Jessie."

"I wonder..." Leslie paused.

Everett tried for lighthearted. "Would you feel better if I took a compass?"

She sighed. "Jessie would be in the ten percent who got it after being vaccinated. I don't want her to expose others on the bus, but maybe everyone on there would be part of the 90 percent."

"Won't be very crowded on the bus this time of day."

"She's in the old school."

Leslie's voice had calmed.

Everett could tell she was no less worried. He had not had Jessie by himself, and he could tell Leslie didn't like the idea. She remembered the qualms more than the others.

"I know. In the back, near the garden." The garden he had designed when Stephen was in kindergarten, after other boys had made fun of him because his dad didn't go to work.

"You have to hold her hand when she gets on the bus."

"Just like I did with you, Missy. We'll call you when we get back here."

WHEN HE WALKED into the

building, Everett expected to see walls lined with colorful drawings and bulletin boards decorated with construction paper and pictures. Instead, a sign informed him that the "Bright Ideas Community Center" was home to twelve small businesses, including the day care center. How times changed.

Still, the smells were familiar as he got closer to the day care rooms. Paste and pineapple juice, the unmistakable aromas of preschoolers.

A woman's voice drifted toward him. "I'm going to look for Jessie May's grandfather again. Be right back." She entered the hallway, eyes on a piece of paper she held. The front of her light blue pants had a large smear of paste and some of her brown hair escaped from a thick braid.

Everett figured she probably spent a lot of time on the floor with her charges. He cleared his throat and her eyes rose from the paper. "You must be the grandpa we've been waiting for."

Spoken in a different tone of voice, the words could have sounded like a mild rebuke. But her smile said otherwise.

"Yes." Everett sensed she expected him to say something more, but when he didn't she gestured he should follow her.

"We have sick room next to the main play room. We can see her through the glass, and she has a little bell to call us. Have to keep contagious kids away from the others, you know."

Everett said nothing. He knew chicken pox to be an airborne contagion. The damage would have been done before the telltale spots appeared.

The woman pushed open the door, and he saw a very subdued Jessie.

"I told you your grandpa was coming. You'll be home in no time."

Everett sat on the edge of the small daybed, next to Jessie. "We're going to my house, Pigeon. After we rest you can go out to the garden for a few minutes if you like." Everett put his hand on her forehead. Not too warm.

"But I can't scratch." Her small brown eyes filled with tears.

Everett assumed the scratching was only part of the reason. No mommy at his house. "You like the bus, don't you?"

Jessie nodded and sat up. Everett knew that the bus was a rarity in her young life of mini-vans and trips to the shopping mall. He hoped it would be a sufficient diversion.

They both turned their attention to the teacher as she picked up Jessie's small back pack and inspected its contents. "Her sweater is in here, but she has on a sweatshirt. She may not need it, as warm as it is."

"Thank you." Everett reached for the pack.

Jessie May stood up. "I'm wearing it."

The teacher smiled as Everett helped Jessie slip her arms into the pack. "Leslie said you wouldn't have children's Tylenol at your house. She called a few minutes ago to say you might want to stop at the store and get some on the way home."

"I like the grape kind," Jessie said.

Her serious expression told Everett that grape was the only option. "I expect they have your flavor." He held out his hand, and she placed a clammy hand in his. Poor little tyke. Everett thanked the teacher and opened the door.

The air in the hallway was cooler than that in the small sick room, and Jessie's somber expression relaxed. "It's nice out here. In that room it was like summer, Grandpa."

"Does the cool air feel good, Pigeon?"

She nodded, her worried expression returning.

"When we stop at the drug store, I'll see if we can buy you something to help make the itching go away."

"That would be good." She took her warm hand from his grasp and wiped her sweaty palm on her jeans. "Does it work fast?"

"I can't say how fast exactly, but

it does help." Everett remembered the pink lotion Sue Ellen applied to children's itchy skin, but he also thought she bathed them in something. He had often sat in the bathroom entertaining a sick child who languished in the tub, but it was Sue Ellen who mixed the concoction that soothed them. Perhaps the pharmacist would know.

As they opened the main door, Everett could see the bus less than a block away. He held the door with one hand so Jessie could pass through, and waved the other at the bus. The last thing he wanted was to sit on the curb for half an hour.

Just as it seemed the bus would

pass by, the driver saw Everett's raised hand and pulled toward the curb. "We have to hurry, Pigeon. We can't keep everyone on the bus waiting."

JESSIE MAY HAD BEEN polite when the pharmacist told her he had made medicines for her mother, and she smiled obediently as the cashier pinched her cheek and told her about the time her Uncle Gerard had toppled the candy display as he tried to climb on it to reach the orange lollipops.

The pharmacist gave Jessie a dose of the grape Tylenol. She inspected her sweatshirt. "I didn't get any on it."

She waited patiently while the

clerk helped Everett find the pink anti-itch bottle and a soothing bath ingredient. Jessie's patience nearly ended when they had to wait almost fifteen minutes in front of the pharmacy for the bus. She didn't even want to look for different types of birds, usually a pastime she liked.

Everett gave up trying to distract her with conversation, and was greatly relieved when he could point out the bus to her. She surprised him when she moved to a seat rather than put the coins in the depository herself. She must feel really bad.

Everett sat next to her. "You've been more patient than your Uncle Stephen and Uncle Gerard when they were your age."

"Of course, they're boys." She drew up her legs and sat cross-legged on the seat next to him.

"You think that's it?"

"Yep. Miss Carson says boys have less of the patience gene than girls do. When they're little, anyway."

Sue Ellen had never liked ascribing behavior or abilities to a child's sex. Everett was pretty sure it was because she had gotten very tired of hearing people say girls were not meant to be the athletes, boys were. Of course, no one talked like that anymore.

"That may be, but I also think you've been an extra good girl for Grandpa because you're my special girl."

She gave him a wan smile. "Thank you, Grandpa." She turned to look out the window and leaned against the pane.

Everett saw tears forming in her eyes. "Just why is it that grape Tylenol is best?"

Her eyes had the 'humor him' look her mother's sometimes did, but Everett thought it was just the typical 'how could you not know' attitude children had when asked an obvious question.

"Because it tastes like grape popsicles."

"I see. It might surprise you to know that I have some of those same grape popsicles in my fridge."

She rewarded him with a real smile and snuggled into him for the rest of the ten-minute ride.

THE PAIN RELIEVER MADE Jessie May sleepy. By the time he had given her an oatmeal bath and swabbed her spots, as she called them, he was exhausted, too. It was much harder than he remembered.

He retrieved the intercoms from the linen closet and placed one in Leslie's old room with Jessie and carried the other one next door to Stephen and Gerard's former room. He would rest for a few minutes. After he called Leslie. She had called when Jessie was in the tub, and he had said he would call her back soon.

When he phoned her, Leslie had more on her mind than Jessie May's chicken pox. "My water broke. And Jimmy's nowhere near here and Jessie has the chicken pox..."

"Which means," Everett raised his voice, "that she'll be over the worst of them by the time you and the baby get home." As he sensed her getting calmer, he added, "You'll handle this just fine, you know."

Sue Ellen would have said that.

"What would Mom do?" Leslie almost whispered.

Her question gave Everett a jolt and he hesitated before answering. "First, she'd probably make some sort of joke about what she was doing when her water broke."

Leslie gave a nervous laugh. "Like in the grocery store for Gerard."

"Yep. How about you, Missy?"

"In the kitchen."

"Hope you hadn't just washed the floor."

"Dad!" She almost giggled. "How's Jessie?"

He was glad he had good news to give her. "Our little Pigeon's sleeping. The bath and medicine helped."

"She'll never sleep tonight."

"That's why I'm going to lie down now. If she's up tonight, I will be, too."

"Umm."

"Don't worry, Missy. I put the

intercom in her room."

"Mom's intercom?"

"The one and only. Well, two of them," he added.

Leslie sighed. "OK Dad, I feel a little better."

"That's good, Missy. How are you getting to the hospital?"

"Jimmy will be back from Iowa City in about twenty minutes. I'm fine until then."

Everett kept her on the phone until Jimmy walked in. It was the first time since Sue Ellen died that they had talked for more than a minute or two at a time. It felt good.

EVERETT AND JESSIE HAD A FAIRLY restful evening. She

awoke about 9 p.m. and ate crackers and chicken noodle soup, and he put more medicine on her spots. Then they watched the "Sound of Music" video.

Soon after she fell asleep at midnight, Jimmy called to say that they had a new baby boy. Stephen Everett.

Everett felt himself flush. "Those are Sue Ellen's initials too, you know."

Jimmy emitted a low whistle. "I'm not sure she's thought of that. I don't think I'll tell Leslie tonight."

"I think I'd wait a few days, too."

Despite the chicken pox, this had definitely been their best day since Sue Ellen died.

CHAPTER NINE

IN THE MONTHS AFTER baby was born, Gerard visited the most, at least twice per week. He said he liked to come, and Everett was glad to see him. Stephen said it was because Gerard was "in between girlfriends," but Everett thought it was because Gerard missed Sue Ellen the most.

Leslie might show her emotions to the world, so people thought she was the saddest, but Everett knew

Gerard was the most forlorn. As the youngest, he had perhaps had more of Sue Ellen's attention as a child and young adult. After all, there wasn't another baby coming along for competition.

Last week, Everett found Gerard staring into Sue Ellen's jewelry box. Everett had asked the four of them if they wanted to have certain pieces, but they all thought it would be better to leave her jewelry together for now.

Leslie wanted Everett to leave all her mother's clothes in the closet, but Everett had been firm. Sue Ellen was practical, and people could use the clothes, unless any of the children wanted something.

Myra took several pieces; she

said she would use them in a painting someday. Perhaps predictably, the boys did not want anything. Leslie did, but she couldn't make up her mind, so Myra picked for her.

Today, Gerard headed for the kitchen to look through Sue Ellen's recipe box. "Dad, do you think we could learn to make some of these?"

"How much of the 'we' means me?" Everett didn't enjoy cooking, and had found several frozen dinners he liked well enough that he rarely made anything more complicated than scrambled eggs. Occasionally meatloaf, which he was partial to and could eat over several days. In fact, it was almost time to start dinner.

Gerard grinned. "I'll do most of it. I just want moral support." He thumbed through more recipes. "I really want to make her poppy seed bread."

The knife Everett was using to peel his apple hit the floor, wood handle first. *Why did it have to be poppy bread?*

"What is it..." Gerard began. He stopped and studied Everett more closely than Everett liked. "Poppy flowers at the funeral, and poppy seed bread. Was it her favorite or something?"

"Favorite? Not that I know of." Everett picked up the knife and paid close attention to the apple peel, making certain it was as thin as possible. He could feel Gerard's stare, and ignored it.

"If I get stuff to make it, can we do it now?"

Everett had no reason to say no, so Gerard left for the store. Everett busied himself with finding the spices and the pan Sue Ellen used when she baked what she called 'designer bread.' Two years ago they had replaced worn cabinets and counter tops with butcher block counters and darker wood cabinets. He liked them, he simply couldn't remember where everything was.

The hand mixer stayed concealed. Gerard could look in the lower cabinets. As far as he was concerned, the only good reason to get on the ground was to work in a garden, and even there he used knee pads now.

Gerard returned in less than half an hour, quite pleased that he had been able to find all the ingredients without asking for help. "Mostly, it was all in the baking aisle. The only thing I had to look for was the poppy seeds, and I finally remembered Mom got it in the canned fruit aisle."

"I didn't realize you shopped with her much."

Gerard paused in unpacking the grocery sack, then continued. "She asked me to take her a few times the last year. Meet her there, actually."

Everett felt as if he'd been

punched in the stomach. "I can't imagine I was so busy?"

"You weren't, Dad. She said you'd be there to carry the bags in."

Everett faced his son. "Then why…?"

"I think she didn't want you to know she was still weak from the chemo. Actually," he placed a carton of eggs on the counter, "she'd been really good the months before…you know…until…"

Everett took the eggs and placed them in the fridge. "Those few months before it came back were some of the best of our marriage."

Gerard nodded. "Not four little rug rats running around?"

"Get that mixing bowl from under the counter, would you? Hand mixer might be there, too."

Gerard knelt in front of a lower cabinet next to the stove and began to push metal baking dishes to one side. Everett figured his son was probably thinking that the cupboards were a lot less organized now.

"Do I need the biggest bowl?"

Everett shook his head. "The recipe is for a single loaf, goes in the pan that's like the one we use for meatloaf."

Gerard deadpanned. "I've had your meatloaf, Dad. Maybe just use this one for bread."

Everett chuckled. "Myra told me to add garlic powder and a bit of brown sugar." He couldn't believe he was discussing recipes with his son. Sue Ellen must be chuckling from heaven.

Gerard's proficiency in mixing ingredients exceeded Everett's so he mostly watched.

"Hey, Dad. I don't need that last egg. Can you put it in the carton?"

Everett picked it up, and promptly dropped it. Yolk spattered the base of a cabinet.

Gerard grabbed a wad of paper towels and wet them. "Sorry Dad. I think I had some cooking oil on my hand when I picked it out of the carton."

"No harm done. I never get all of them used before the date on the carton." Everett moved to the stove and set the oven to 350 degrees.

WHILE THE BREAD BAKED, Gerard deftly scrambled eggs and Everett made toast. Breakfast for dinner. When they were little, the kids had begged for it every Sunday night. As long as pancakes were included.

The timer dinged and Gerard rose from the kitchen table to check the bread. "I'll do the dishes, Dad."

Everett collected their plates and stood. "I'll put them in the sink for you."

The floor must have been slippery because of the egg. As he pitched forward, Everett had the familiar sense of spiraling out of control.

CHAPTER TEN

DURING THE AMBULANCE RIDE, Everett reassured Gerard at least five times that the accident was no one's fault. Finally, the EMT told Gerard to focus on his father rather than his feelings.

Everett liked the expression. He turned his head from the comfortable pillow, and tried to ignore the continual jostling as the ambulance hit bump after bump. If the EMT hadn't put a sort of bubble cast on his broken wrist, the trip would have been agony. "Gerard, look at me."

He did.

"It's no big deal. If I'd broken my ankle, it would be hard to get to the garden. This is nothing."

Gerard frowned. "That's because we haven't had to explain it to Leslie yet."

Everett laughed and winced. His head hurt, but it wasn't the worst headache he'd ever had. Gerard had told the EMT that Everett's brief spiral into unconsciousness was because he hit the metal handle on the stove drawer where Sue Ellen's large frying pans rested. Of course, he didn't mention the pans.

When he had awakened, Gerard

had already called 9-1-1. In between the few tears that coursed down his cheeks, Gerard kept telling Everett he would be fine. Everett knew that. His most immediate concern was calming Gerard.

"You need to tell Leslie we had a good laugh about it."

"A laugh?" The EMT asked.

At maybe twenty-five, Everett thought the man hadn't had time to learn that humor helped almost anything. "We have to convince my oldest daughter that this is a blip, nothing more."

The EMT grinned. "So the floor was slippery? Tell her it was a blip from a drip."

Gerard gave a weak smile and

Everett wished he had a favorite begonia to give to the man who had lifted him off the floor.

Leslie was at the ambulance entrance when they arrived. Everett remembered that she had a friend who worked in the ER.

"Oh, Dad. I was so afraid something like this would happen."

Everett's gurney was pushed past her, but he sensed her accusatory look in Gerard's direction. "Not a big deal, Missy. Really."

Gerard's tone was firm. "Dad says a broken wrist won't keep him out of the garden."

An authoritative woman's voice said, "You two can sit on those chairs over there while we assess your father."

"But," Leslie began.

"Or out in the lobby," the stern woman said.

Everett felt himself relax as the EMT wheeled him into a private examination room. No need to put up a good front for children. His wrist hurt as if it had been hit by a wild pitch at one of the softball games Sue Ellen coached.

A different woman's melodious voice said, "I'm just going to put some more pain medicine in the IV that the EMTs started."

"Thank you." Everett forced a smile. "You aren't exactly offering me Thanksgiving turkey."

The woman laughed and

Everett opened his eyes to look at her. She was almost as pretty as…

The poppies extended to the horizon. If a person had to pick a place to die, this field was fine. If only he could convince Benny to stop talking about death. The lack of water made him hallucinate. He kept thinking he heard German bombers coming. But that couldn't be…

"Mr. Jenkins? Are you awake?"

"Sort of," he mumbled.

"The nurse wants to know if it's okay if your children come in."

Everett opened his eyes. A woman with a stethoscope was shining a flashlight in his eye. She was not the camp medic. The hospital, of course. He had broken his arm. Or wrist. "I suppose. Not for long."

The doctor, a woman about fifty with what Myra would call a stylish haircut, smiled at him. "From the exam when you came in and what I see now, I don't see signs of a concussion. We'll probably keep you overnight to be sure."

"Thank you." Everett wanted to sleep, and if Leslie stayed long, he'd absorb her nervous energy.

Gerard walked in front of Leslie as they entered the examining room. Usually his son would let one of his sisters precede him. Probably wanted to take in the situation before Leslie could get more upset.

"Okay, you two." Everett was surprised at how weak he sounded, and raised his voice. "I'm going to be okay. Just a broken bone."

Gerard stood on the right side of his gurney and tapped him on the shoulder. "I know, Dad."

Leslie, on the left, added, "Gerard said it's just a blip from a drip."

Everett grinned. Gerard had been able to calm his sister. Or at least convince her to act that way. "Good way of putting it." He focused on Leslie. "Now, Missy, you need to get home to your little ones."

"I think I should…"

Everett made a shushing sound.

"You aren't going to put the cast on me. I like to see you, but Gerard is here."

Gerard nodded. "He's right, Leslie. It's going to be a lot of waiting and fifteen minutes of getting a cast put on. I'll call you."

Everett had an idea. "Gerard will call you, and you can let the others know." His eyes began to droop. "Plus, I need a nap."

He caught a few words that Gerard and Leslie exchanged before Benny appeared again.

Benny grinned through parched lips. "You said they'd come." He pointed at the circling plane, and together they watched someone parachute from it. Everett hoped they had water.

"WANT AN ICE CHIP, DAD?"

Everett opened his eyes to see a haggard Gerard leaning over his hospital bed. Funny, last he remembered he'd been on a gurney. "Sure. Got any lemonade?"

Gerard smiled and moved a spoon toward Everett's mouth. "I can't believe you pretty much slept through the docs putting on that cast."

Everett glanced toward his hand. A purple cast, with a heart drawn on it in black ink. "Myra was here?"

"Still am."

Everett turned his head. "You picked the color?"

She smiled. "It's Jessie's favorite, you know."

As the ice made its way down his throat, Everett felt himself fully awaken. He swallowed. "Good idea." He nodded at the cast. "Your artwork?"

"Of course."

Gerard offered him more ice. "Myra made a deal with the devil. I mean, our beloved sister."

Everett figured Gerard would use the phrase in front of his oldest sister, so he simply looked from his son to daughter. "Since I don't see her, I take it you convinced Leslie to stay home."

"And Stephen," Myra said. "I will sit here until you go to sleep tonight. Gerard will pick you up tomorrow morning."

"You don't have to," he began.

Myra pointed to a chair. "I have sketch pads and a skirt I'm hemming. No big deal."

"Good plan." He switched his gaze at Gerard. "I'm sorry I frightened you so, Son."

"I'm good, Dad. No more baking for me."

Everett shifted his weight from one shoulder to the other. "I enjoyed that. We'll do it again. Now go home."

GERARD, LOOKING RESTED, ARRIVED at the hospital at seven-thirty the next morning. Everett had eaten, and wanted to get home. The hospital staff had been helpful, even kind, but they woke him every hour or so to take his blood pressure. Something about being sure he didn't have a concussion. He wanted to get home to nap.

"You look better, Dad."

"Thanks. Less groggy, since some of the medicine's worn off."

"Good. They didn't actually put you to sleep. The doctor gave you a shot to deaden your arm, and some sort of sedative before they set your wrist."

Gerard warmed to his topic. "It was kind of cool to watch. They had your x-ray on this light board thing and a sleeve already on your arm. Then he kind of moved your wrist 'til he had it where he wanted. Then a resident started wrapping this wet goo that became your cast."

Everett glanced at his cast again. He'd eaten with his other hand, and had barely paid attention to the purple creation. "Not too heavy."

"Fiberglass." Gerard lowered his voice. "I think the doc is sweet on Myra."

"Gracious."

Gerard grinned. "She liked him, too. She told him she'd be the one taking you in for a check-up."

"That's Myra. Do you know when we can leave?"

"Not sure. I stopped at the desk when I came in. They said a doctor would be around to release you in an hour or so."

A rap on the door led Gerard to say, "Come in."

Stephen poked his head around the door and smiled. "You look better than I expected."

"I really am fine."

Gerard frowned lightly. "And if any more eggs fall on the floor, I'm scrubbing for ten minutes."

Everett waved his good hand. "Your mother kept trying to get me to cook better. I should have studied harder."

Stephen sat in a chair near the window. "You want to stay at home, right?"

Everett's nod was firm. "Of course."

Gerard frowned again. "You're

going to have to be firm with Leslie."

"Bottom line, it's up to me."

His sons nodded. At almost the same time, they said, "She's just a worrier."

They all laughed. It felt good.

Everett sobered. "I'll stay in the house until you have to waste your time checking on me a lot. And no more falling."

CHAPTER ELEVEN

EVERETT HAD EXPECTED THE first anniversary of Sue Ellen's death to be an especially difficult day. Instead, he had wakened to beautiful late fall weather, feeling peaceful.

With the cast removed from his arm a couple months ago, he could spend part of the morning cleaning the kitchen for the family dinner. Then he headed down to the gardens. As the sun grew lower in the sky, he drew the rake over his bed of dead annuals and scooped the detritus of a summer of zinnias, begonias, and marigolds into a brown recycling bag.

Putting the garden to bed for the first time without Sue Ellen. If some form of corporeal heaven existed, she was sitting up there glad not to have to hold the bag.

He mentally went over a to-do list for late afternoon. His children, their spouses, and both of his grandchildren were coming for supper. He smiled. The newly married Myra referred to his fall a few months ago as "the lucky break."

He had to agree. Dr. Thomas – "call me Tom" – Rooney was

rooted in science as firmly as Myra was in art, and they appreciated their differences immensely.

Everett went back to his list. Vacuum the living and dining rooms, place dishes and silverware on the dining room table, and take the poppy bread out of the freezer. He and Gerard had made it last weekend, as a sort of tease to Leslie.

A glance at his watch said it was time to finish in the garden and get cleaned up for dinner. He stopped at a bed that had remained protected from frost by an overhang from the back porch. Plenty of fall mums to use for a dining table arrangement.

THE DOORBELL RANG THAT EVENING as Everett, freshly showered, walked from the second floor to the entry foyer. Judging from the incessant peals, Jessie May had beaten her parents to the porch.

Everett opened the door and was rewarded with a toothy grin from the almost-kindergartener, as Jessie had taken to calling herself. She skipped into the house. "We have a surprise Grandpa."

Her father called from the back door of the family's car, where he was wrestling with the baby's car seat. "The surprise is a secret, remember, Jess?"

She rolled her eyes, clapped her hands in delight, and raced to the sliding glass door that led to the back porch. "Is my butterfly bush gone?"

"Afraid so, Pigeon." Everett called this as he stepped onto the front porch to hold the screen door open for Leslie, who carried a diaper bag and cookie tin.

"Hi, Dad. You look great."

He took the cookies and kissed her cheek. "I'm about to be even better."

"At least better fed."

Everett held the door for Jimmy and their now six-month old son. Leslie and Jimmy were still coming up with nicknames for their boy. They didn't want to call him Stephen or Everett, believing it would be confusing. Everett had been tempted to say only confusing as long as he was around, and he was getting up there. But Leslie wouldn't laugh at that.

Jessie almost bounced to the foyer to find Everett. "Can we go down for just a minute? Only one minute?"

Leslie gave Everett an imperceptible shrug.

Everett smiled. "Okay, Jess, for a minute. Grandpa wants to be here to greet the other guests."

She ran to the sliding door and flipped the tiny switch that unlocked it. "They aren't guests. They're family."

Jimmy chuckled behind him as Everett slid the door shut and he and Jess headed down the stairs.

Jessie made for the now barren butterfly bush, paused briefly, and then ran to the remaining mums. "I told Mom there would still be color."

Everett smiled. "This time of year, we look to the leaves for color."

She craned her neck to study the tallest oak tree and its orange leaves. "I like the red ones better."

"Maple trees lose their leaves earlier."

"And they're the only reds?"

He shrugged. "Around here, mostly." He wished Sue Ellen were here to see their wonderful granddaughter explore the gardens.

She stood on the brick walk and

turned full circle. "Where are the Sue Ellen Blues?"

Everett had his first heart pang of the day. "Your Grandma's favorite flowers, did you know that?"

He led her to his most special roses, and watched her inspect a bush. One unopened bud sat on a bottom branch, protected by leaves that had blown into the base of the bush.

Jessie bent to stare at it. "Will it bloom?"

"Too late, I'm afraid."

"Can we take it inside?"

"Sure." Everett stooped and pinched the thin bloom from its branch and handed it to her. "Don't hold it too tight, or it'll pretty much fall apart."

She stared at it, then looked up. Her eyes held tears about to spill onto her cheeks.

"What is it, Pigeon?"

She whispered, "I only remember Grandma in bed."

Everett smiled and pointed to a nearby cement bench. "That's because you were little. You've seen pictures of her when she was healthy."

As they walked to the bench, Jessie drew the back of one hand across an eye. "She was next to my horse."

Jessie's horse? "Ah. When you rode the carousel at the fair. I took that picture."

From above, voices drifted

down. It sounded as if Gerard and Stephen had arrived. Probably not Myra, or her laughter would bubble around the house.

Jessie's face brightened. "You took extra pictures, because I scrunched my eyes at the sun!"

Everett smiled at her delight. "See, you do remember. It would be okay if you didn't. You'll always hear stories about your Grandma."

The door above slid open and Jimmy called, "Pop? Jessie? Come on up you two."

"Be right there," Everett replied.

Jessie sighed and looked at her bud. "I have to be extra good tonight."

Everett took her hand. "You're always good."

She grew solemn. "Mostly. Sometimes I forget when the baby's asleep."

"So did your Uncle Stephen, when Myra and Gerard were asleep."

Jessie let go of his hand, and bounded up the steps, likely to ask Stephen about his behavior.

Everett entered the house and blinked as he adjusted to change in light level. Then he looked at the dining room, laden with a feast. "Goodness. You all have been busy."

Jessie tugged on Everett's arm. "Mommy baked a turkey. Turkey is your favorite."

Everett moved to Leslie and kissed her cheek. "As busy as you are. Thanks, Missy."

She nodded. "I'm learning not to pay attention to unmade beds and dishes in the sink."

"But she always remembers to clean the diaper bucket," Jessie chimed. She stared around the room, uncertain why her parents and uncles were laughing so hard.

Everett recovered first. "She takes after your Grandma."

Jessie pointed to the table. "See the boxes?"

"Not yet, Jess," her father said.

Gerard glanced from the table to Everett. "A surprise in a minute, Dad."

Jess looked crestfallen, so Everett winked at her. Something about those small boxes looked familiar.

Myra's cheery hello from the foyer stole his attention. He walked behind Stephen to shake Tom's hand and kiss his younger daughter.

Tom's voice had a booming quality when he wasn't in the hospital or his office. "How's my favorite patient?"

Everett smiled. "I'm shaking your hand, aren't I?"

Myra served as a sort of master of ceremonies during dinner. Each child had a story or two about Sue Ellen, most funny, occasionally poignant. Everett had been looking forward to what Gerard called Sue Ellen's anniversary dinner, but he hadn't expected the stories. His stomach clenched and he began to wish dinner was over.

Stephen seemed to pick up on Everett's quieter mood. "Okay, I think we need Leslie stories."

"You mean how when Mom and Dad had their backs turned she'd make me eat her peas?" Gerard asked.

Jessie's eyes widened. She looked at her father. "Really?"

Laughing, he shrugged. "I didn't know her then."

Leslie laughed, too. For a time after Sue Ellen's death, Everett didn't think she would ever laugh again. Her second child seemed to have brought a slightly more relaxed perspective on life.

"Jess," Stephen called to her. "It

wasn't just Gerard. Ask Myra."

Myra's mascara had already run down her cheeks, so more watering made no difference. "Carrots," she choked.

Leslie raised both hands in the air. "Enough already."

"Mom, can we open the boxes?" Jessie asked.

Each of his children looked at one another, and Tom finally said, "I'd like to see them."

Myra stood. "Everybody clear the table. We can do dishes after."

As instructed by Leslie, Everett stayed seated, occasionally smiling as he heard Leslie instructing her brothers about how to wrap leftovers or told them not to save what she termed a miniscule piece of pie. Apparently Gerard ate it, because he said something Everett could not understand. Gerard's mouth sounded full.

He drew a deep breath. Sue Ellen would be proud. Not just at how she had raised their children, but at how they had handled her death. He was proud of them.

His eyes strayed to the three boxes now sitting on the credenza next to the dining table. One red, two dark blue. A small leather album now sat beneath them. Probably vinyl, not leather. He hoped they hadn't made him some sort of photo album. He wasn't ready for an evening of photos or videos of Sue Ellen.

The kitchen door opened, and

his children and sons-in-law filed out, led by an excited Jessie May. "It's time, Grandpa! It's time!"

Everett patted the chair next to him. As Jessie sat, they both turned to look at the bassinet in the corner. Stephen Everett had awakened. He wasn't crying – yet. Jimmy picked him up as the others seated themselves around the table.

Everett waved at the baby. Leslie had told him that his little namesake couldn't distinguish shapes from a distance, but Everett always looked for ways to engage the child.

Stephen cleared his throat, and they all quieted.

That was a first.

"Okay, Dad," he began. "We

weren't one-hundred percent sure what you'd think of this, but we ordered you something special."

"Three sets of cufflinks?" Everett asked.

"Not hardly," Gerard said. Everett couldn't say why, but he thought his youngest son looked subdued.

"Something extra special," Myra added.

Jessie slipped out of her chair and went to stand near the boxes.

Everett glanced at them, and realized why their shape and color looked familiar. He hoped he was wrong.

Stephen looked directly at Everett. "So, we know you don't like to talk about what you did in the War, and we respect that."

"But after we talked to those men at, you know, the funeral, we looked it up," Leslie said. "Or, Stephen did."

Everett felt himself shaking. *Please, God, not the qualms.*

"It turns out," Stephen continued, "that the Army will reorder medals if people lose theirs."

"I'm not sure," Everett began, and stopped. Twice through the years, Sue Ellen had asked if she could tell their children something about his war experiences. Especially Africa, as she said.

Both times it was when the boys were upset because other kids made fun of Everett not working.

Not working and occasionally keeping score at their softball games. Usually the moms kept score and the men coached. He had told Sue Ellen not to bring it up with them, and she had reluctantly agreed.

Apparently their children had needed to know. He told himself he didn't have to talk about the War. He could listen for a minute, and ask them to change the subject.

The room quieted, and everyone looked to Everett.

"Go ahead," he said, "but let's not dwell on this." If he said nothing, it would be over fast.

Gerard seemed to let out a breath. Perhaps, Everett thought, his son knew Everett would not like to be confronted with his wartime past. Good for him.

Stephen opened each of the thin boxes and placed them to face Everett. He listed their contents. "You received the
Combat Infantryman Badge,
Air Medal, and
Bronze Star Medal with Valor."
The sharp pinging sounds would not stop. Metal on metal. Bullets hitting parked planes and metal pots. Everett almost reached up to cover his head with his arms. That had been the problem that night. It was supposed to be safe. Their helmets were in their tents. He'd been using his for shaving water that morning.

Everett shook his head slightly.

"You got these where?"

Myra cleared her throat. "We weren't sure how to go about it, so we asked the congressman's staff. You know, the office is in town. They knew exactly what to do. They gave us request forms, and they got them."

Leslie shifted the baby, which she now held, from one shoulder to the other. "He wanted to present them personally, but we explained you might not like that."

"He, uh, wrote you a letter of thanks," Gerard added.

"Good of him," Everett murmured. He gripped the edge of his chair, wanting to stay upright.

"But the best part," Stephen continued, "is the album."

"Album?" Everett asked.

Stephen opened the roughly six-by-nine photo album and turned it to face Everett. "The lieutenant and sergeant, they sent photos of their kids and grandkids. And I guess a few of other men you served with. They said none of these kids would have been born if you hadn't saved them all that night."

The room began to tilt. Or was it the foxhole? Benny! Benny wake up! Everett stared into his friend's unseeing eyes.

From a distance, someone asked, "Dad? Are you okay?"

Everett sat up straighter, his gaze on the picture of poppies on the dining room wall. Myra had moved from her chair to stand next to him, her hand on his shoulder. Everett looked up at her, and then at each of his silent family members in turn.

His gaze rested on Jessie May, whose beautiful lips formed a silent o. He smiled at her. "Grandpa's okay, Pigeon. Some of my memories are happier than others."

She grinned, almost slyly. "I looked at the pictures."

"When?" Leslie asked.

Jessie's tone grew confident. She probably knew she wouldn't be scolded in front of her family. "It was on the coffee table. You didn't say not to." She looked toward Everett. "You want me to show you my favorite one, Grandpa?"

Looking at these photos was the last thing Everett wanted to do. But instead of slamming shut the album, he pointed to the chair next to him. "Sure thing, Pigeon."

Quicker than a rabbit in his garden, she was at his side, and gestured that he should sit back in his chair. "I want to be on your lap, Grandpa."

For fully ten minutes, the only sounds were Jessie May's comments on the photos and her baby brother's suckling noises as Leslie fed him. Jessie seemed to like any picture that showed a child with a person she judged to be a grandparent, and was especially fond of the few dogs that appeared next to their owners.

She shut the album with a thud. "Do you know all these people, Grandpa?"

He shook his head. "I met a few of the oldest people, many years ago. I hadn't seen any of them for, oh, thirty years or so."

"Except the tall man," she said.

"The tall man?"

She nodded. "He came to Grandma's funeral, remember?"

"Of course." Everett glanced across the table and met Jimmy's eyes.

Jimmy stood. "Come on, Jessie. You can help me put some cookies on a plate."

She slid off Everett's lap. "But we already had our sweets."

Everett couldn't help but smile.

Jessie had long since learned she would not get every cookie or cupcake she asked for.

"I know," Jimmy said. "But it's been a while since we had pie. Maybe your Uncle Gerard wants a cookie."

When the swinging door to the kitchen shut behind Jessie and Jimmy, Leslie cleared her throat. "We can't imagine how difficult it was for you, Dad."

"And you never need to look at any of this again," Gerard said. "It just...it meant a lot that those men came, you know, for Mom. When they said you saved them all, well..."

Myra interrupted her brother, and spoke softly. "We're so proud of you, Dad."

Everett opened his mouth to speak, closed it, and tried again. "I appreciate that." His gaze swept the table. "From all of you. But you weren't there, in that War, I mean. We were all willing to take a chance. For each other. To live."

He stopped. If he kept talking, he'd break down. Benny didn't live.

Leslie's voice was a whisper. "But it was you, Dad. Just you. You saved them all." She nodded at the now closed album. "Mr. Brimmer said these are just a few of the people who were born because of what you did that day."

Everett swallowed. "I'm glad this is important to you. But I've spent a lot of years forgetting. I don't believe I'll talk about this again."

"We get it," Stephen said. "But for us, Dad, knowing all this, it's a lot of pieces falling into place."

Everett stared at him. Falling indeed.

THE END

ABOUT THE AUTHOR

Elaine L. Orr primarily writes traditional or cozy mysteries – those without a lot of gore that feature an amateur sleuth. She began *Falling Into Place,* literary fiction, almost fifteen years ago. The story needed to feel just right.

Her Jolie Gentil cozy mystery series has ten books and a prequel. *Behind the Walls* was a finalist for the 2014 Chanticleer Mystery and Mayhem Awards. The first in the Iowa River's Edge series, *From Newsprint to Footprints,* came out in 2015, and the Logland series began with *Tip a Hat to Murder* in 2016.

She also writes plays and novellas, including the one-act play, *Common Ground,* and the novella *Biding Time.*

www.elaineorr.com

OTHER BOOKS
BY ELAINE L. ORR

Elaine's books are generally self-published, via Lifelong Dreams Publishing and are at all online retailers. They are available as ebooks, paperbacks, large print, and audio books. Your local bookstore or library can order the books.

Jolie Gentil Cozy Mystery Series

Appraisal for Murder
Rekindling Motives
When the Carny Comes to Town
Any Port in a Storm
Trouble on the Doorstep
Behind the Walls
Vague Images
Ground to a Halt
Holidays in Ocean Alley
The Unexpected Resolution
Jolie and Scoobie HS Misadventures (prequel)

River's Edge Mystery Series (Annie Acorn LLC Publishing)
From Newsprint to Footprints
Demise of a Devious Neighbor

Logland Mystery Series
Tip a Hat to Murder

NONFICTION
Monett (Arcadia Publishing)
Words to Write By: Putting Your Thoughts on Paper
Writing in Retirement: Putting New Year's Resolutions to Work
500+ Hashtags for Writers
Orr, Campbell, Mitchell, Shirley Families: Descendants of Paul Orr and Isabella Boyd in Ireland and America

http://www.elaineorr.com

Check the index on her blog, Irish Roots Author, for articles on reading, writing, publishing, and whatever musings are going through my head.
http://elaineorr.blogspot.com

If you are considering publishing yourself, you may also be interested in my self-paced online classes. One (Thinking Through Self Publishing) is free.
Information is at my website.

Whatever you do, enjoy reading!

www.ingramcontent.com/pod-product-compliance
Lightning Source LLC
Chambersburg PA
CBHW070842120626
46556CB00002B/843